Our Field

Based on a story by Juliana Horatia Ewing
and retold by Berlie Doherty

Illustrated by Robin Bell Corfield

PictureLions
An Imprint of HarperCollinsPublishers

For Dan and Tom
BD

For Sue, Oliver and Ruth
RBC

Author's Note
It is over a hundred years since this story was first told,
and in those days there were lots of wild flowers for people to pick.
Nowadays they're very rare, so we aren't allowed to pick them,
but must leave them where they are for everyone to enjoy.

Robin Bell Corfield drew the following people to use as characters in this book, and would like to thank them
for their invaluable assistance: Jonathan and Danielle Mayes; Alison, Lauren and Helen Hulbert; Anne Mosley;
and the pupils at Great Dalby Primary School, Leicestershire. Also thanks to Vintage Years, Costumiers, Leicester.

First published in hardback in Great Britain by HarperCollins Publishers Ltd in 1996
First published in Picture Lions in 1997
9 10
ISBN: 0 00 674865 1
Picture Lions is an imprint of the Children's Division, part of HarperCollins Publishers Ltd,
77-85 Fulham Palace Road, Hammersmith, London W6 8JB.
Text copyright © Berlie Doherty 1996. Illustrations © Robin Bell Corfield 1996.
Printed and bound in Singapore.

· Chapter 1 ·

THE DOG WHO NEARLY DROWNED

We never knew who had drowned Pierrot, but it was Sandy who saved his life and brought him home. Pierrot wasn't at all nice to look at when we first saw him, though we were very sorry for him. He was wet all over, and his eyes wouldn't open. You could see his ribs, and he was all dark and sticky. But he dried a lovely yellow colour, and his ears were like black velvet. We never knew what kind of dog he was, except that he was the best possible kind.

"Well, he's very nice," Mother said. "But we can't keep him. Don't look at me like that! We can't afford to keep him."

We were all very miserable. So we had a meeting in our den under the table. Pierrot came too.

"Suppose we offer to give up sugar to help pay for his keep?" Sandy suggested. It was a very generous offer, coming from him, because Sandy loved sweet things. But he loved Pierrot more.

"Well," sighed Mother when we told her our decision, "I suppose so." We all cheered.

"But who's going to pay for his licence at the end of the year?" she said. "I can't."

We went back to our den.

"It's not fair," said Richard.

"I wish we had a fairy godmother," said Sandy. "All these godparents we've got, and none of them are fairies!"

"I don't believe in fairies anyway," I said. "We've got to do this on our own."

"We could save up," Richard suggested. "All our halfpennies and pennies."

"Even our sweet money," Sandy promised.

"All right," I said. "And we'll keep them in a stocking."

Chapter 2

SEARCHING FOR A DEN

We could have done with a fairy
godmother, all the same. Apart from
helping us to pay for Pierrot's licence,
we could have done with one to find
us a decent den. We were fed up with
people putting their feet into our table
house, and when we moved into the
outhouse we'd just set it up nicely
when a new load of wood was
delivered and covered up everything,
our best oyster-shell dinner service
and all.

It was one day in early May –
a very hot day for the time of year,
which made us all a bit grumpy
– when Sandy came home from
school grinning his head off.

"I've got a fairy godmother,"
he said, "and she's given us a field."
As I said, Sandy loved eating, especially
sweet things. He used to save things from
meals to enjoy afterwards, and he almost always had a piece
of cake in his pocket. He brought a piece out now and took a
large mouthful, laughing at us over the top of it.

"What's the good of a field?" asked Richard.

"Great for dens," mumbled Sandy.

"I'm tired of dens," I said. "It's no good. We always get turned out."

"It's a new place," Sandy went on, and took a triumphant bite of cake.

"How did you get there?" asked Richard.

"The fairy godmother showed me."

"You shouldn't talk with your mouth full," I said.

Sandy laughed and said, "I'll show you, if you like."

Of course Pierrot came too. Sandy led us along the lane and over a stile and through a gate and over another stile and round a field...

...and over another stile and there he stopped.
"Here it is," he said. "Our Field."

· *Chapter 3* ·

THE BEST FIELD IN THE WORLD

The great heat of the day was over. The sun shone low down and made such wonderful shadows that we all walked about with grey giants. It made the green of the grass, and the cowslips down below, and the snowy blossom on the blackthorn hedge, and Sandy's hair, and the mist behind the elder-bush, so yellow, so very yellow, that for a minute I really believed in Sandy's fairy godmother, and thought that everything was turning into gold.

"I'm sorry, Sandy," I said, "for telling you not to talk with your mouth full. This is the best field in the world."

"Sit down," said Sandy, and we all sat under the hedge. He turned over on to his stomach and fumbled under the leaves.

"Look," he said. "Violets."

"And bluebells," said Richard, looking at the green tops.

"As thick as peas," said Sandy. "This bank will be all blue when they come out. And there's fiddleheads everywhere, turning into ferns. Wait till the may blossom's all out! And there's a wren's nest in there –" he rolled over on to his back and looked up. "Can you hear that lark? This will be a great field for a kite, don't you think? But wait a bit."

After every new thing that Sandy showed us, he always finished by saying, "Wait a bit", because there was always something better still.

"There's a brook at the bottom. We can paddle in it. But wait a bit. Look at this hedge. It's like shelves. We could play at shops here – but wait a bit."

He ran across the field towards the opposite hedge, and then stopped. "No. I'll save it," he said, and sat down with his arms round his knees and rocked himself backwards and forwards. He was bursting with satisfaction.

"Sandy!" we shouted. "What is it?"

He laughed and stuck out his tongue, and then he turned all his pockets inside out into his hands, and mumbled up the odd currant, saying, "Guess!" between every mouthful.

But when there wasn't a crumb left in the seams of his pockets, he jumped up and said, "It's a hollow oak tree!"

He ran and we ran to the other side of Our Field. I had read of hollow oaks, and once I dreamed of one with a witch inside, but we'd never had one to play in.

We were nearly wild with delight. From the
field it looked all solid, but when we pushed
behind, on the hedge side, there was a door.
I crept in, and it smelt of wood, delicious damp.
The light came in from the top, where the fern
hung over like a fringe. Richard came in,
and Pierrot, and we all agreed. It was
the very best thing in Our Field.

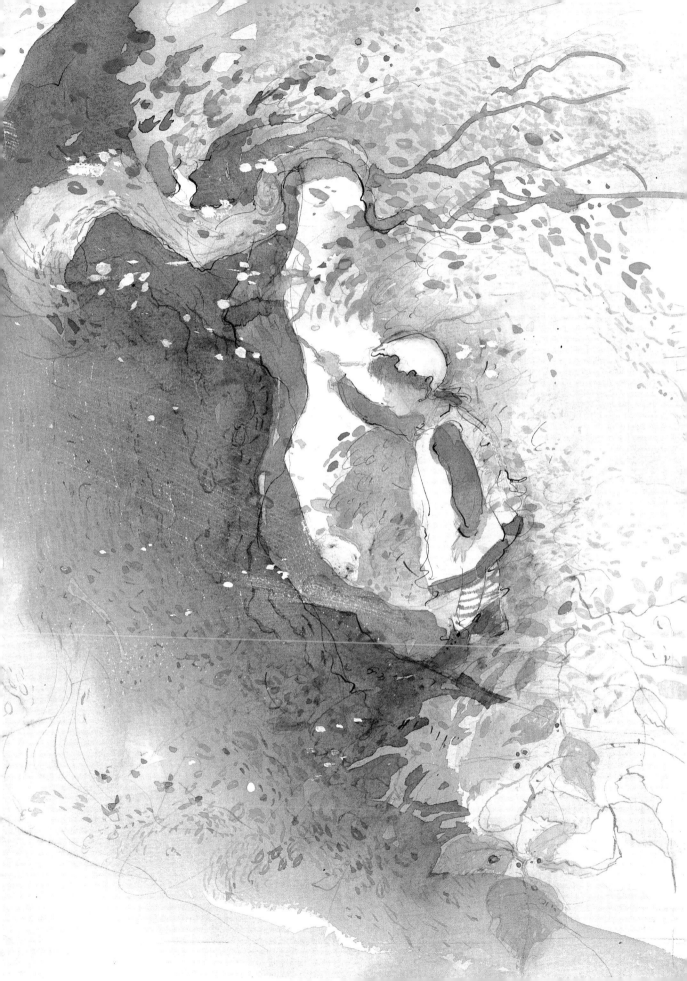

· *Chapter 4* ·

ALL SUMMER LONG

Pierrot loved the field as much as we did. What he liked best were the little birds. I think he knew that it was Our Field and that he was watchdog of it, and whenever a bird settled down anywhere he barked at it and then it flew away and he lost it, and by that time another had settled down. He never caught a bird but he would never let one sit down if he could see it.

We played all kinds of games in Our Field. Mostly shops, on that wonderful hedge-bank. Sometimes I sold mosses, from the ten different kinds of moss by the brook. Sometimes I was a jeweller and sold daisy chains and pebbles and bracelets made of berries, and necklaces of oak apples. Sometimes I was a grocer, and sold earth-nuts and mallow-cheeses and mushrooms.

My favourite shop was the florist's, because I loved making bouquets and sprays from the flowers, and little umbrellas out of rushes. Richard and Sandy were my customers and paid with money made of elder-pith, cut into rounds. They lived by the brook and were wine merchants, and made cowslip wine in a tin mug.

We played at castles and houses, too. We hung Richard's cap on the stile post, just as the Queen has a flag hung out at Windsor Castle when she's at home.

When we wanted a change, we pretended to pack up and go to the seaside. First we made jam from the wild strawberries and packed it to take with us, in case the children got hungry. Then Sandy and I bathed Pierrot in the brook, which he loved, and Richard sunbathed on the bank and spied at us through a telescope made of an elder stem. When it wasn't being a telescope, it was a flute.

We were never disturbed. Birds, and cows, and men and horses working in the distance, they didn't disturb us at all.

We were very happy that summer. The only
thing that worried us was the thought
of Pierrot's licence money.

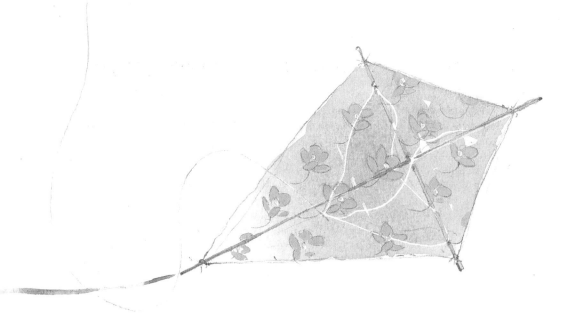

Months passed, and we still hadn't saved it. Once we got as far as two-pence halfpenny, and then one day Richard came to me and said, "I need some string for my kite. Please lend me a penny out of Pierrot's stocking."

"All right," I said, "as long as you pay it back."

And the next day Sandy came and said, "Pierrot lent Richard a penny; I'm sure he'd lend me one too."

"All right," I said.

And then they said it was ridiculous to leave a halfpenny there all on its own, so we spent it on acid drops.

I started dreaming horrible dreams about Pierrot having to go away because we hadn't saved his licence money. I used to wake up and cry till the pillow was so wet that I had to turn it over. And one day I found Sandy alone in Our Field with Pierrot in his arms, crying, and feeding him with cake.

"Oh Pierrot," he sobbed. "We don't want to lose you! We don't want to lose you!"

I can't bear to see anyone crying. I'd much rather cry myself.

"Please don't Sandy," I begged him. "I'm sure something will turn up."

And the very next day, it did.

· Chapter 5 ·

A CHANCE TO SAVE PIERROT

We were in school. The schoolmaster rapped on his desk and said, "Silence, children! I have good news for you."

We all sat up to listen.

"A lady wants to give a special prize to children at the village show this year. The prize will be for – the best arrangement of wild flowers. And the prize will be – five shillings!"

There was a gasp and a cheer from all the children. I hardly dared look at Richard and Sandy. Five shillings! It was exactly what we needed for Pierrot's licence money!

"Silence, children!" The schoolmaster waved his arms at us. "You must be able to give these flowers their English names."

"Easy," I whispered.

"Silence! And there will be a second prize for the best collection of mosses. The lady wants to encourage a taste for natural history."

"What's natural history?" everyone was asking.

"Silence!" the schoolmaster cried.

I squeezed Sandy's arm. I thought I should never finish my lessons that day for thinking about Pierrot.

"They must come out of Our Field," I told the boys, "every single one. We know all the names of them. One of you can help me, and the other one can do the mosses from the brook – we can easily make up names for those!"

Richard made me a box. We put damp sand in the bottom, and then lovely clumps of feather moss, and into that I stuck the flowers. They all came out of Our Field, and they had such lovely names – orchid and harebell, meadow sweet and buttercup, dog rose and cranesbill, speedwell, marigold and cornflower. I called out the names for Sandy to pass them to me, and it was like a song. And in between I called out for labels to write the names on, and for grasses – cock's foot and foxtail and shivering grass. I had nothing to do but put the colours that looked best together next to each other, and make the grass look light, and to pull up bits of moss to show well. And at the very end I put in a label, 'All out of Our Field'.

And then I wasn't a bit happy with it, but Richard praised me so much that I cheered up. And I told him that his mosses looked lovely. But oh! I was so nervous.

ALL OUT OF OUR FIELD

· *Chapter 6* ·

THE DAY OF THE FLOWER-SHOW

The flower-show day was very hot – I didn't think it could be hotter anywhere in the world than it was in the field where the show was; but it was even hotter in the tent.

We nearly didn't get in at all. We didn't know you had to pay to get in. We looked at each other in despair.

"Well," said the ticket-lady, seeing our faces, "I'll let you in free, as you're competitors."

It was hard work getting through the crowds of grown-ups. We kept seeing tickets with '1st prize' and '2nd prize', and struggling up, only to find they were big floppy garden flowers, or fruit that you weren't allowed to touch, or vegetables. I got sick of the sight of vegetables. I don't think I'll ever like big red potatoes again. It makes me feel sick with heat and anxiety just to think of them.

We struggled slowly all round the tent. We saw all the cucumbers and onions and lettuce and big round potatoes time and time again, and then we saw an old lady with a table of wild flowers in front of her. And there it was, right at the front, my collection!

It had a big label on it marked '1st prize'! And next to it was Richard's tray of mosses, and that had a label too: '2nd prize'!

And I gripped one of Sandy's arms and one of Richard's and shouted, "We've done it! We've paid for Pierrot!"

Chapter 7

THE FAIRY GODMOTHER

There was two and sixpence left over. We never had such
a feast! It was a picnic tea, and we had it in Our Field.
I thought Sandy and Pierrot would have died
of cake, but they were none the worse.

The strange thing was, the old lady came too!
She just arrived in the middle of our picnic,
and sat down with us. It was as if she
knew about the field all the time.

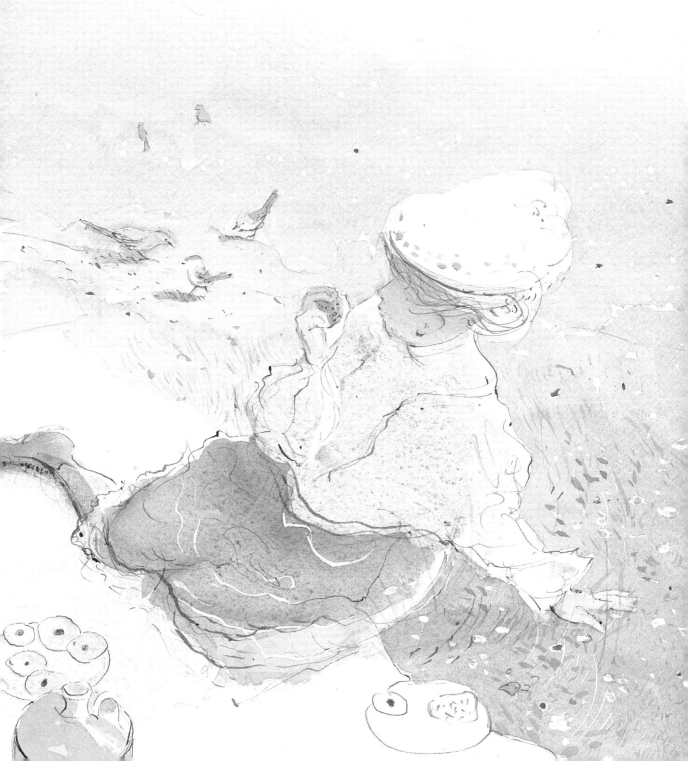

She brought some nuts and
she paddled in the brook,

and she even got inside
the hollow oak, though it
was really too small for her.

I don't think I've ever known anybody so kind. Just as she was leaving I said anxiously, because I didn't want to seem rude, "You won't tell anybody about Our Field, will you?" And she winked. We all tried to wink back, but only Richard could do it properly.

"I used to play here myself," she said, "a long time ago."

She climbed over the stile.

"But whose field is it?" I shouted.

And that's when I began to nearly believe in fairy godmothers, after all.

"Yours," she told us.
"It's Your Field now. It really is."